Boats on Big Rivers

Written by Tracey Michele

Picture Dictionary

ferryboat

motorboats

paddleboat

Read the picture dictionary. You will find these words in the book.

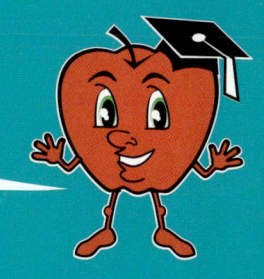

raft

rowing skiff

tugboat

This is a raft.
People in rafts
can go fast on big rivers.

5

These motorboats are on a big river. People go up and down the river in motorboats.

dinghy

cabin

This boat is a rowing skiff.
You can see rowing skiffs on some big rivers.
People race them on rivers.

bow

oar

This is a tugboat.
Tugboats push
and pull things
on big rivers.

barge

containers

You can see paddleboats on some big rivers. People take river trips on paddleboats.

steam

paddle wheel

13

This boat is a ferryboat.
You can see ferryboats
on big rivers.
People and cars
go on ferryboats.

funnel

deck

15

Activity Page

1. Draw a tugboat pulling a barge of containers on a big river.

2. Label:
   tugboat   bow   cabin
   barge   containers   river bank

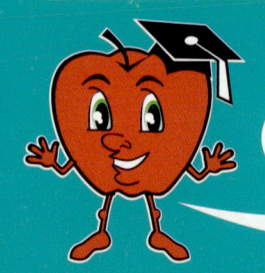

Do you know the dictionary words?